D1101963

ADELE GERAS

The Magical Story House

Illustrated by Joanna Walsh

MACDONALD YOUNG BOOKS

For Jan Mark

Text copyright © Adèle Geras 1996
Illustrations copyright © Joanna Walsh 1996

This edition first published in Great Britain in 1996
by Macdonald Young Books
an imprint of Wayland Publishers Ltd
61 Western Road
Hove
East Sussex
BN3 1JD

Reprinted in 1998

Typeset by Backup... Creative Services, Dorset
Printed and bound in Belgium by Proost International Book Production

British Library Cataloguing in Publication Data available

ISBN 0 7500 1883 6

Chapter One

"I'm eight," said Simon. "I don't need a babysitter. I could stay at home by myself while Mum is at work."

He was struggling to keep up with his brother, Lou, who was striding along the pavement as if they were going somewhere important.

"I'm not a babysitter," Lou said. "I'm an actor. You're just helping me today, that's all."

"But," said Simon, "I don't like cleaning houses. If you're an actor, why aren't you acting?"

"I'm waiting," said Lou, "for the right

 part, and meanwhile I enjoy cleaning people's houses. You'll enjoy this one too, you'll see."

Simon snorted. He had perfected a collection of different snorts and this one meant: why can't my brother have an ordinary job like everyone else? If he worked in a garage, I could help with the cars. Simon's daydream of oily rags and bits of machinery was interrupted. Lou had said something interesting.

"Did you say 'haunted'?" Simon asked. "I didn't hear you properly. Are we going to clean a haunted house?"

"Certainly," said Lou. "I always say a haunted house should be just as clean as an ordinary house. I feel quite strongly about it."

Simon ignored this remark.

"*How* is it haunted? Have you been there before? What happens?"

"Oh, all the usual things. Groans and so forth. I believe there are bones under the floorboards in the lounge, and ghostly music floating down the stairs, and then of course there's the locked room. No one ever goes there."

"Why not?" Simon whispered.

"Well, for one thing," said Lou, "it's locked."

"And for another?" Simon blinked.

"No one has told me," Lou said in a graveyard voice. "Better not to ask, that's what I always say."

Simon was feeling nervous. "Are we nearly there? Does Mum know you're taking me to a haunted house?"

"Oh, yes," said Lou. "It's perfectly safe."

"How do you know?" Simon asked.

"Nothing's ever happened to me, has it?"

"I suppose not."

"Here we are, then," said Lou at last. "This is it."

"It doesn't look haunted at all." Simon was disappointed. Where were the darkened windows and the ivy-covered walls? What about the door-knocker in the shape of a gargoyle? There was no overgrown garden, no mysteriously-twitching curtains. It was simply a tall, narrow house with a bright

red door and laurel bushes on each side of the path.

"It's ordinary," he said at last.

"You mustn't judge by appearances," said Lou, and he took a key from his pocket and opened the door.

"It's me, Mrs Martin," he shouted up the stairs. "It's Lou, come to clean." There was no answer.

"Is there somebody here?" Simon asked.

"Only Mrs Martin. I expect she's busy upstairs. Or she could be asleep, of course. She is a very old lady. I'm going to the kitchen to get stuck in. You look around."

Chapter Two

Simon looked around and decided that Lou had been pulling his leg. In this house, he was perfectly sure, there were no bones buried under the floorboards in the lounge. The hall was painted white, and hung with pictures, and there was a vase of yellow tulips on a small table beside the telephone. He wasn't even slightly frightened. I'll prove it's not haunted, he thought. I'll go into the lounge and see what's in there.

The room was full of armchairs and sofas covered in velvet, and there was a large mirror on the wall over the mantelpiece. A fat, stripey ginger cat was lying curled up next to a fat, stripey cushion on the windowseat. Simon smiled.

"My brother's mad," he said to the cat, who had opened one green eye to see what was disturbing his morning snooze. "He says there are bones under the floorboards."

"Not that I know of," said the cat in a furry, purry voice. "Although I myself have hunted down a good many moths here, so I daresay there are the remains of wings and what have you."

Simon sat down on the nearest armchair.

"You can speak," he squeaked.

"Certainly," said the cat. "Most cats can speak. It's simply that there are very few people worth making the effort for."

"I can't believe it... I must tell Lou..." Simon jumped up and ran to the open door. He shouted in the direction of the kitchen:

"Lou... Lou... come here at once... there's a cat here that can talk."

Lou came into the hall with his arms full of dusters.

"He's in here, Lou. Come and see."

Lou approached the windowseat, smiling.

"This is Hobbes," he said, tickling the cat under his chin. "Ooz-a-lovely-pusscat-then?"

"You do see, don't you," said Hobbes, "why I don't speak to just anybody? I mean, really. One would think I was dimwitted."

"There!" Simon said. "Did you hear that?"

"Hear what?" Lou looked puzzled.

"Leave him, dear boy," said Hobbes, "to his dusting and polishing. We will do quite well on our own, just the two of us."

"Nothing," said Simon. "It's OK. You get on. I'm going to stay with Hobbes."

"Well, if you get fed up, come and find me. I can always get hold of another cloth for you."

Lou left the room and Simon snorted. This snort meant: as if I could ever be fed up with a talking cat for company. Hobbes jumped off the windowseat and stretched himself.

"I shall show you round the house," he said. "This house has many interesting features."

"Is it haunted? My brother said it was haunted."

"In a way, I suppose it is." Hobbes began a careful licking of his left back paw.

"Shrieking skulls? Headless house-maids? Rattling chains? Bones? Bats? Anything like that?"

"Oh, no," Hobbes yawned a wide, pink yawn. "Nothing as vulgar as that. No, our house is more enchanted than haunted. Let me show you. Have you noticed the wallpaper? Most people don't see it, because it is so faded, but there is a pattern there. Can you make it out?"

"It's rather nice," said Simon. "It's like a very pale jungle... leaves and creepers and things."

"Try over there," said Hobbes, looking towards the corner of the room furthest away from the door.

Simon walked into the corner and tried to put one hand flat on the wall, but the wall had gone, and he felt as though he were reaching into a hedge. Stems and leaves scratched at his arm.

"My arm's gone into it… into the wall."

"Follow it," said Hobbes. "Follow it into the jungle."

"Come with me," said Simon. "I'm scared by myself."

"I'll be here when you get back," said Hobbes. "The tigers will look after you."

"Did he say tigers?" Simon wondered aloud.

"Welcome to our jungle," said a voice, and Simon found himself face to face with a tiger wearing a smart white suit and a pith helmet.  The jungle looked more or less like all the jungles he'd imagined, but surely the animals shouldn't be dressed and able to speak?

"I expect you've come to tea," said the tiger. "It so happens that this is a very good day to come to tea, because it's my son's birthday. So good of you to visit us…"

Over morning coffee, as Lou called it, Simon told him all his adventures.

"...and then we had birthday cake and crackers to pull, and it was getting quite late, so all the tigers took me back, and I stepped through the jungle wallpaper and there I was, back in the lounge with Hobbes again."

He took another bite of his biscuit.

"A vivid imagination," said Lou, "is a great gift. Now I must get on, so off you go, back to your furry friend for another good natter. Who knows where he'll take you next?" Simon snorted again, and this time he meant: it was all true and I know you don't believe me, but I don't care, so there.

Chapter Three

Simon went to look for Hobbes, and found
him at last, lolling about on the first floor
landing.

"My brother didn't believe in the tigers,"
Simon told him.

"The tigers," said Hobbes, "will be there
whether he believes in them or not. So it
really doesn't matter."

Simon wasn't paying attention. "Listen,
Hobbes," he said, "I can hear something.
There's music coming from somewhere."

"From Miranda's nursery," said Hobbes.
"I expect it's her musical box."

"Who's Miranda?"

"Miranda," said Hobbes, "is a girl. We can go and visit her if you like."

"Yes, please," said Simon. "Let's go and find her. I never knew there was a girl living here."

He followed Hobbes up to the first floor, wondering why this Miranda, whoever she was, hadn't come downstairs to see them when she heard them come in. Perhaps she was very shy. Was she related to Mrs Martin? Why hadn't Lou mentioned her?

"Knock at the door," Hobbes said. "I shall wait out here." He folded his legs under his body and sat on the first floor landing like a fat, ginger Sphinx, staring at Simon out of unblinking eyes. Simon knocked.

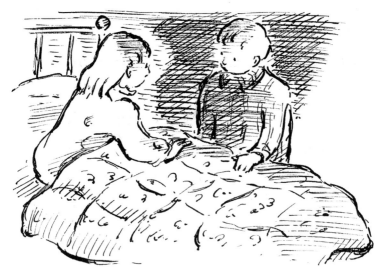

"Come in," said a girl's voice, and
Simon went in.

"Hello," he said, sounding much braver
than he felt. "My name is Simon."

"How do you do, Simon," said the girl,
who was sitting up in bed. "I'm Miranda."

"Are you ill?"

"I was," she said. "But I'm better now.
I'll be able to get out of bed soon."

"I like your room," said Simon. "It's…"
He couldn't think of the right word. It
wasn't like his room at home nor like any of
his friends' rooms. There were no toys in it

he could recognize: no Lego, no computer games, no Barbie dolls or Action men. There was no radio, or cassette player, and no model aeroplanes. Instead, this Miranda had a rocking-horse, some dull-looking books, a few dolls, a humming-top and a whole collection of pictures that she was sticking into a scrapbook.

"I collect footballers," said Simon. "And cars. But I've never seen any pictures like this before."

He didn't say so, but they looked soppy to him: rosy-cheeked children, and kittens and puppies and brightly coloured bunches of flowers. One scrap had fallen on the floor and Simon picked it up and put it absent-mindedly in his pocket. It was a picture of a vintage car, full of jolly people in fur hats and muffs.

"Come and see my musical box," said
Miranda. "Isn't it lovely?"

"I heard the music," said Simon. "From
downstairs. Will you play it for me again?"

Miranda opened the box, and inside was
a small, glass swan, going round and round
on a piece of mirror that was meant to be
a lake.

"That's terrific," said Simon, and went
to look out of the window. "Hey! You've got
a great garden. Do you ever go on the
swing?"

"I will in summer," said Miranda, "when I'm quite better." She yawned. "I'm very tired now, but thank you so much for visiting me. Will you come again?"

"I'd like to," said Simon, but Miranda had closed her eyes. He shut the musical box, and went to find Hobbes.

Chapter Four

The cat was nowhere to be found. Lou was cleaning one of the bedrooms. Simon asked him: "Have you seen Hobbes?"

"No, sorry," said Lou. "Why don't you look on the top floor?"

Simon went upstairs calling Hobbes's name, but there was no sign of him.

"Are you looking for my cat?" said a voice behind him. "He's with me."

An old lady was standing in the doorway of what looked like an attic room. This was probably Mrs Martin, Simon thought.

"I'm sorry if I disturbed you," he said. "I'm Lou's brother, Simon. He's downstairs doing the bedrooms."

"And you don't like cleaning, do you?" said the old lady. "I'm Vanessa Martin, and I don't blame you. I could never stand it myself. Do come in and sit down. I call this room my study, even though it's years since I've done any work here."

Simon went in. There was nothing in the
room but a huge desk covered with papers,
and a comfortable-looking chair next to it.
The old lady sat down.

"You will have to sit
on the floor like
Hobbes, I'm afraid."

"I don't mind," said Simon.

"Have some barley-sugar," said Mrs Martin. "Do children nowadays eat barley-sugar? It tastes delicious and it's such a beautiful colour. When I was a girl, we used to buy it in long twisted sticks, and it's still my favourite. And tell me what you have been doing. Have you been bored?"

"Oh, no," said Simon. "Not at all. I've been talking to Hobbes."

"Indeed?" Mrs Martin looked at him strangely. "He doesn't talk to everyone, you know. What has he been telling you?"

Simon hesitated. He didn't want to mention the tigers, or Miranda. Mrs Martin would probably be just as scornful as Lou was. He said: "All sorts of things," and then, to change the subject, he added: "Lou says there's a locked room…"

"There is," said Mrs Martin. "I'll unlock it for you, if you'd like to see what's inside."

Simon felt fear fluttering round in his stomach like a small bird.

"I don't know," he said. "It depends what's in there."

"Only books, I'm afraid," said Mrs Martin. "All my old books live in there. In boxes, most of them, but I have been going through them lately, so there are a few lying about that you could look at."

"Thank you," said Simon, wondering how soon he could get away from Mrs Martin and talk to Hobbes again. It wouldn't be polite not to go and look at her books, not now that she'd offered to open the locked room for him.

"There you are, young man," said Mrs Martin as the door creaked open. "I'll leave you to get on with it. Do call again whenever you fancy a chat and some barley-sugar."

"Thank you," said Simon. "I will."

Chapter Five

The first book Simon picked up was called 'The Tigers' Tea-party'. He looked at the pictures. That was just like... there was the wallpaper... there was the tiger in his white suit and pith helmet. The little boy in the book could have been him. Simon closed the book and looked at the cover again. 'The Tigers' Tea-party' written and illustrated by Vanessa Martin.

"Quite right," said Hobbes, who had reappeared silently at Simon's feet. "That's our Mrs Martin. She was, long ago, a maker of books and pictures. This whole house is full of them. Haunted by them, if you prefer to put it like that." Simon picked up another book: 'Miranda's Musical Box.' He knew, even before he opened it, exactly what Miranda's room would look like.

"Next time you come," said Hobbes, "I will show you the garden. That's full of stories, too. My favourite is the one

about the magic swing. Or if you'd rather, we have a pirate ship in a bottle on the kitchen windowsill, and

an aquarium which is home to the tiniest of mermaids. That's in the dining-room."

"Simon!" Lou's voice came drifting up the stairs. "We have to go home now."

"Coming!" Simon shouted back. "I'm just saying goodbye to Hobbes."

On his way downstairs, Simon knocked on Miranda's door. There was no answer. She must still be asleep, he thought, and opened the door. The room was quite empty. Simon ran down to the hall, where Lou was waiting for him.

On the way home, Simon put his hand in
his pocket for no particular reason, and
pulled out a small scrap of paper. It was the
picture he had picked up in Miranda's
room, the one with all the jolly people in
furry hats.

"What's that?" said Lou.

"Nothing," said Simon. "It isn't anything."

Later, when they were nearly at home, Simon said: "You were right. That house *was* haunted."

"What did I tell you?" said Lou. "It isn't every day, after all, that you bump into a speaking cat!" He winked at Simon and touched the side of his nose with one finger. Simon snorted, and this snort meant: I know something you couldn't possibly imagine. He followed Lou up the stairs to the front door.

Look out for more exciting titles in the yellow Storybooks series:

Gilly the Kid by Adèle Geras
Gilly the Kid is a cowgirl. She's got no time for school – she and her pony Biscuit are on the trail of a real live baddy!

A Magic Birthday by Adèle Geras
Maddy is really looking forward to her birthday party, but there is one thing missing. Will it spoil her special day?

Emily's Legs by Dick King-Smith
At first, nobody noticed Emily's legs. Then, at the Spider Sports, everyone began to ask questions.

Tall Tale Tom by Anne Forsyth
Tom loved making up tall stories – even though they always got him into all sorts of trouble!

I Want That Pony! by Christine Pullein-Thompson
Sophy is desperate to own Flash, the pony that lives down the lane. But Flash already has an owner, who doesn't want to give him up.

Alice Alone by Shirley Isherwood
Alice and her little brother are staying with their grandad on his farm. But one evening grandad doesn't return home. What is Alice going to do?

You can buy all these books from your local bookseller, or they can be ordered direct from the publisher. For more information about Storybooks, write to: *The Sales Department, Macdonald Young Books, 61 Western Road, Hove, East Sussex, BN3 1JD*